DOG DIARIES

FALA

DOG DIARIES

#1: GINGER
A puppy-mill survivor in search of a *furever* family

#2: BUDDY
The first Seeing Eye guide dog

#3: BARRY
Legendary rescue dog of the Great Saint Bernard Hospice

#4: TOGO
Unsung hero of the 1925 Nome Serum Run

#5: DASH
One of two dogs to travel to the New World
aboard the *Mayflower*

#6: SWEETIE
George Washington's "perfect" foxhound

#7: STUBBY
One of the greatest dogs in military history

#8: FALA
"Assistant" to President Franklin Delano Roosevelt

DOG DIARIES

FALA

BY KATE KLIMO • ILLUSTRATED BY TIM JESSELL

RANDOM HOUSE 🏠 NEW YORK

The author and editor would like to thank Dr. Bryan Blankfield, Department of Communication Arts and Sciences, Pennsylvania State University, for his assistance in the preparation of this book.

All rights reserved. Published in the United States by Random House Children's Books, a division of Penguin Random House LLC, New York.

Random House and the colophon are registered trademarks of Penguin Random House LLC.

Visit us on the Web! randomhousekids.com

Educators and librarians, for a variety of teaching tools, visit us at
RHTeachersLibrarians.com

Library of Congress Cataloging-in-Publication Data
Klimo, Kate.
Fala / by Kate Klimo ; illustrated by Tim Jessell.—First edition.
pages cm. — (Dog diaries)
ISBN 978-0-553-53490-0 (trade) — ISBN 978-0-553-53491-7 (lib. bdg.) —
ISBN 978-0-553-53492-4 (ebook)
1. Fala (Dog), 1940–1952—Juvenile literature. 2. Roosevelt, Franklin D. (Franklin Delano), 1882–1945—Juvenile literature. 3. Dogs—United States—Biography. 4. Presidents' pets—United States. I. Jessell, Tim, illustrator. II. Title.
E807.1.K59 2016 973.917092—dc23 [B] 2015004109

Printed in the United States of America

10 9 8 7 6 5 4 3 2

First Edition

For Sandy

—K.K.

To the brave and steadfast Allies of WWII
and their loyal and loving dogs,
who were at their sides

—T.J.

CONTENTS

Fala listens to the Boss's speech on the radio.

BIG BOY

'Tis a bonny day in the month of July. My mistress, Mrs. Augustus G. Kellogg, is enjoying a spot of tea with a lady friend on the patio of her estate in Westport, Connecticut. I am having a dandy time with a rubber bone. I toss it in the air and catch it between my teeth with a smart *snap*.

"What a darling boy!" our visitor gushes.

At four months of age, I am well used to the fawning of strangers. They cannot help themselves.

I am a fuzzy ball of black fur with a head too big for my body. Still, this woman gets my dander up. Who is she calling darling? Hoot, man! *Darling* is for wee lap doggies with ribbons in their topknots—not for such as me, a fine Scottish terrier with the diehard Highland blood running through my veins! The name is Big Boy. I am so called not for my size—which some have the brass to call runty—but for my personality, which is huge and powerful.

I detect a trespasser in our midst: a furry gray one. I dash over to where my dear daddy lies sleeping. I pounce upon him. *Wake up!* I yip.

Whah? he mutters, lifting his head groggily.

Squirrel! I bark.

Why didn't you say so in the first place? He leaps to his feet. *Where? Let me at it, laddie!*

This way! I say, leading the charge.

Together, we run pell-mell across the lawn. Round and round the big pine we chase the fuzzy intruder. The tip of her tail is nearly between my teeth when, suddenly, up the tree trunk she shoots. She chatters down at us.

I rear up, tearing the bark to shreds in my frustration. *Be thankful that Scotties cannot climb trees, missy, else you would be chattering out the other side of your saucy little mouth!*

Forget it, Son, Daddy says, giving his coat a sound shake. *Squirrel, one; Scottie, naught.*

Just wait, you furry gray gink, I growl.

Back to the patio I trot with my head held high. I did not catch her. But I have shown the wee thing who is boss. And, what is more, I have given the ladies an eyeful of my superior form.

The mistress says, "You've always wanted one of Peter's pups. This is the perfect opportunity.

Why don't you take him home with you?"

What is this I hear? Has the mistress gone daft?

The lady friend sips her tea. "Oh, I'd love to," she says, "but I'm in New York City half the time, and I'd hate to lock up a spunky little pup in an apartment. He needs a big house and a lawn to romp on."

She has got that right! Whew! I settle down with my head on my paws. But I keep one eye open. The lassie has a scheming look about her, and she is not to be trusted. Sure enough, the next words out of her mouth are: "Come to think of it, I've got the perfect home for him!"

"Really?" the mistress asks.

Och, no! Do not listen to her, Mistress!

"The White House!" the lassie says.

Whatever the White House is, mention of it sends the mistress's teacup clattering into her saucer. "Goodness me! Does the president even *want* a dog? It seems to me there was an unfortunate incident in the newspapers a while back."

"You mean when Major, his German shepherd, bit Senator Caraway? Oh, the president had to send that poor creature away. Not *every* dog is cut out for high office. But I have a feeling that Big Boy here was born for it. He would never bite a United States senator, would you? Not even a Republican."

I pull my lip away from my teeth and growl softly, not that the lass takes the slightest heed.

"But he hasn't been trained," the mistress says. "A dog in the White House must be on his best behavior at all times."

"I'll train him myself," says the lass with a sly wink my way. "I'll teach him to do tricks. It will be fun, won't it, Big Boy?"

I huff into my paws. *These people have a lot of*

nerve, tossing me around like a blithering chew toy!

Take it like a dog, Big Boy, Daddy says gruffly. *We go where the humans send us, and we do it without complaint. Besides, a dog without purpose? Why, he might as well learn to purr and be a cat.*

The lady friend reaches down and pats my head, like we are old friends. "Don't be sad, Big Boy!" she says to me. "Look at it this way: your country needs you. What with fighting the Depression and keeping the New Deal on track, campaigning for a third term, and coping with the war in Europe, the president's got a world of trouble. A charming little roly-poly pup like you will help lighten his burden, I just know it. What do you say?"

Something in her voice as she says this gives me pause. I speak here, dear reader, not about the kind that are furry but the kind that make you sit up and think. And what I am thinking is that this man sounds big and powerful. He would have to be, wouldn't he? To be running an entire country?

Suddenly, I feel ashamed of myself. So far, my life has been one long puppy romp, interrupted by the occasional squirrel chase. But now fate—in the form of this bonny lass—has presented me with an opportunity. I, Big Boy of Westport, Connecticut, will go forth and help the president run this great nation of ours.

I place my muzzle in her hand to show her I am the dog for the job. She can count on Big Boy to get it done.

And that is how it comes to pass that I go home with one Miss Daisy Suckley.

The Suckley family estate in Rhineback, New York, is filled with strange smells and creaking noises. At first, I neither eat nor play. My wee rubber bone gathers dust. Nights are the worst, when the house is as dark as a waistcoat pocket. I huddle beneath Miss Daisy's bed and whimper. Miss Daisy seems to understand. Every so often, she reaches down and gives me a nice firm pat. And each morning, as the sun rises, my spirits rise a wee tad higher.

Breakfast helps. She fixes me boiled eggs. Soon, my appetite returns, along with my natural high spirits. I begin to flip the rubber bone in the air and catch it again. Miss Daisy starts giving me small chunks of raw meat for dinner. And then the lassie brings out the biscuit tin.

"All right," she says one day on the porch. "Big Boy, you give me your paw. And I'll give you a biscuit."

Och! Has she gone off her head? My paws are mine to use as I see fit. I cannot be bartering with them. Perhaps if I stare hard enough at the biscuit, she will give it up.

She lifts my paw and shakes it. "See? That's all you have to do, Big Boy. Pick up your paw and shake with me. Then you'll get your biscuit."

It does not take Big Boy long to catch on. When my paw goes up, I get the biscuit. It is as easy as jumping off a rock.

The game gets harder, but I keep at it. Before very long, the lass has me sitting down, rolling over, prancing on my hind legs, and lying down—all for a crunchy biscuit. I also learn to say *please,* which means barking on command. If my *please* comes out too loud and rowdy, I'll not get the biscuit. I have to say it *oh, so quietly.* "Use your White House Voice," is how the lassie likes to put it.

Every afternoon, I play with Tammy and

Smudge. Tammy is one of my own, a fine Scottish terrier. I have not the foggiest idea what Smudge is, nor does she. She is naught but a frizzy pile of fur with a wee sharp nose poking out. We are mates,

the three of us, and we run in a pack. Woods and streams surround the estate. We scamper hither and yon, giving chase to birds and chipmunks and rabbits and squirrels. Once we come upon three deer. Tammy and Smudge turn on their heels and head for home. But Big Boy is all for chasing Big Game. I follow the deer as they leap and caper, ever deeper into the woods, until, by some devious trickery, they vanish. By then I am in the bosky depths of the forest.

It is not until after sundown that I spy the lights of Miss Daisy's porch. She falls to her knees and gathers me up in her arms.

"Big Boy, where have you been? You had me worried sick. I thought you were lost. I promised the president I'd bring you over for a visit tomorrow."

I bark. She has to understand that every so often, a Scottie needs a wee ramble.

The next morning, she spends hours combing the burrs out of my coat, sighing and lamenting. But she cannot be all that vexed, because no sooner are the burrs removed than off we go for a ride in the country.

Say, have you ever seen a dog hanging out the side of a moving automobile? To open your mouth and taste the rushing wind on your tongue. To hear it whistling through your ears. To feel it blowing the fur back from your eyes and muzzle. Hoot, man! Dog Heaven.

At length, we sweep down a long pebble drive. The lines of tall trees on either side are alive with birds and squirrels. At the end of the drive, Miss Daisy halts before a big stucco house. A flag with stars and stripes hangs over the front door.

"This is Hyde Park, the president's house," she explains to me carefully. "When he's not working at the White House in Washington or resting in Warm Springs, Georgia, he's usually here. He was born here, reared here, and prefers it to anyplace else on earth. If you're a good little dog, you'll get to stay and share it with him."

She gets out of the car and comes around to open the door for me. I leap out and follow her up the front steps.

A man in a white jacket greets us at the door.

"Hello, Whitehead," Miss Daisy says. "I've brought a little friend to meet the president."

"Afternoon, Miss Suckley. The president's expecting you . . . and Big Boy, too."

Och! The smells that hit me as I step through the door! Paper and dust and pencil shavings and ink and old books. And through it all, the smell of feathers and fur and dried blood and bone. These last come from the big glass-fronted cases filling the front hall. On shelves behind the glass are wee beasties and birds. Big birds. Little birds. Birds perched on twigs and birds sitting on nests. Birds with their chests puffed, singing their birdie hearts out.

I go to the glass and sniff. At first, I think they are frozen in fear. Then it hits me. *Big Boy,* I tell myself, *these beasties and birdies? They are all of them dead.*

Miss Daisy smiles. "Don't get excited. The president doesn't hunt and stuff animals any- more. That was just a boyhood hobby. He collects stamps now."

Then she ducks behind a nearby door. I scam- per after her into a cozy room overlooking the drive. A broad-shouldered man sits in a chair with big wheels. Round spectacles glint on his narrow face, and his head is wreathed in smoke. With his chin jutting out, he clenches a long cigarette holder at a jaunty angle in his mouth.

"Cousin Daisy!" he calls out in the high, reedy voice I will soon adore. "It's grand to see you."

"Mr. President," says Miss Daisy with a sweep of her hand, "meet Big Boy."

2

THE SHAGGY SCOTSMAN

The president throws back his head and roars with laughter. "He looks like a mop! Or a feather duster!" says he.

I march right over and growl in indignation. *Blow it out your bagpipes, buster!*

Chuckling, he leans over and lifts me in his arms. He scratches me behind the ears. Och, but it feels grand! I lick his chin.

Miss Daisy stands nervously by the door. "I

think I'll let you two get better acquainted," she says. "Behave, Big Boy," she adds before leaving.

I lick the president again to show him how well behaved I can be.

A young woman soon interrupts us. She comes in, sniffling into a hankie. "Oh, Mr. President! I'm afraid I've made a terrible mistake."

"What is the problem, child?" he asks in a gentle voice, his hands stroking me all the while.

"Oh, it's too, too terrible for me to say!" she moans.

"Tell me your troubles. My shoulders are broad."

She breaks down and tells her tale of woe. When she finishes, the president says he will make a few calls and straighten out the mess. She goes away, all smiles.

Next, two men come in, scowling. They sit

down, and both begin to talk at once. One of them is Professor Sam Rosenman. The other is Harry Hopkins. They call the president Boss. They talk to the Boss about a speech he wants to make to some soldiers on something called Armistice Day. The Boss plans to begin the speech, he says, by talking about the history of democracy. The other two groan. This will bore the stuffing out of his listeners, they say. But the Boss knows what he wants to say and how he wants to say it. He sets me down on the floor, then waves his arms about as he explains. Professor Sam and Mr. Hopkins nod.

"We're on it, Boss," they say as they leap to their feet and dash out the door.

A young lady marches in next, carrying a great stack of papers, enough to housebreak a whole kennel of Scotties.

"Boss," she says. "I need you to sign yesterday's

correspondence when you get the chance."

"I have the chance now, Tully," says the Boss. "Give them to me."

From beneath the desk, I hear the scratching of pen against paper and dare to peer out at Tully. Is she the Boss's wife? I smell a mate lurking some-where beneath this roof, but so far I have not laid eyes on her. But no, Tully is not the one. She smells of paper and ink. She cocks her head and peers back at me.

"Why, hello there, little fella," she says. "Aren't you a furry ball of cuteness?"

Och! Cuteness! What of Nobility? What of Loyalty? Bravery? I will show her just how brave I am. I creep out from beneath the desk. She kneels and strokes me.

"Does Mrs. Roosevelt know you're thinking of getting a new dog?" she asks.

"I wrote and told her," the Boss says. "She approves. Eleanor thinks that you and Daisy need someone to help look after me while she's traveling."

Tully giggles. "He looks like a grumpy old man," she says.

"He has a certain air of . . . dignity," says the Boss as he signs papers.

"Say, don't you think he could do with a haircut, Boss? He looks a bit scruffy for the White House."

The Boss snorts. "He's better groomed than some congressmen I know. He's a shaggy Scotsman, and he'll stay that way."

"Is that true, Big Boy? Are you a shaggy Scotsman?" Tully asks me.

"And he won't be Big Boy much longer," the Boss says, with a twinkle in his eye. "If I decide to keep him, I'm renaming him after my notorious Scottish ancestor Murray the Outlaw of Falahill."

Och! To think of me answering to that great mouthful of steaming haggis. (That would be *sheep guts* to you.) Over my cold, dead wee Scottish body!

"That's a mighty big name for a small dog," Tully says, laughing.

"I'll call him Fala for short," the Boss says.

I sniff. *Fala. Hmmm.* Well, Fala I can probably stomach.

All afternoon, as people come and go, I stay under the desk. Every so often, the Boss reaches down and gives me a pat. I wait for him to take me out to do my business, as Miss Daisy is teaching me. Just when my puppy bladder is full nigh on to bursting, some kind soul comes and takes me outside. I am brought back and returned to my place under the desk.

That night, the Boss eats dinner off a tray in that same room. It does not escape my notice that on the tray is a bowl of raw meat. I stare up at him until he stops chewing and looks at me.

I growl, *You cannot fool a Scotsman. That bowl of meat is meant for yours truly.*

"Oh, so you're hungry now, are you?" he asks in a teasing tone.

I lick my chops and stare meaningfully at the bowl.

"Sit," he tells me.

I sit.

"Lie down," he says.

I settle onto my haunches.

"Dance," he says.

I rise up onto my hind legs and do my best canine interpretation of the Highland Fling.

"Say *please*."

I bark in my softest White House Voice, *Please.*

"Good dog," he says. "I see my cousin trained you well." He sets my meal on the floor on top of a bit of newspaper.

I clean the bowl in seconds.

Licking my chops, I wait to see what happens next. Ever the optimist, I hope for a biscuit. Even dogs deserve dessert. Instead, he rings a bell. A strapping black man named Prettyman comes and rolls the Boss down the hall. So that's what the big wheels are for! I hop up onto the Boss's lap and hitch myself a ride. Prettyman pushes the chair into a wee wood-paneled room.

The door closes, and the room begins to creak and grumble and groan. The floor beneath us shifts. Something terrifying is afoot! I bark sharply to alert the others.

"Easy," says the Boss. "It's only an elevator."

"Dog'll have to get used to elevators, Mr. President," says Prettyman.

"That and trains and boats and, sooner or later, maybe even army transport," says the Boss. "Not to mention noisy crowds, exploding flashbulbs, buzzing microphones, and pesky reporters." The Boss chuckles, and Prettyman joins in.

The door opens, and we roll out of the elevator. To my amazement, I see that we are in a whole new hallway! That is one mighty tricky little room, that elevator! Prettyman pushes us in the chair and stops outside a large bathroom.

"You'd better wait outside . . . unless you want a bath," the Boss says.

I leap off his lap and back away. Soon, through the closed door, I hear the sounds of splashing and the Boss talking and laughing with Prettyman.

I feel an itch, and I reach for it with my hind leg, the leg going *thump-thump-thump* on the floor. Suddenly, I look up and see a tall, proud woman glaring down at me. I stop thumping and stand at attention. Perhaps she has a biscuit for me.

She leans down and whispers, "If my son insists

on having a dog, I don't see how I can object. But you had better not bring any fleas into this house."

Och! So it is going to be like *that,* is it? I can tell you this: if I had any fleas, they would jump off my back and flee in sheer terror. She holds my eyes until I look away. Satisfied that she has made her point, she turns on her heel and disappears back down the hall.

I am greatly relieved to see the Boss coming out of the bathroom, smelling sweet as a newborn bairn, with his hair slicked back and his nightclothes on.

In the Boss's bedroom, another man is waiting. He and Prettyman make a chair of their hands. The Boss puts his arms around their shoulders.

"One, two, three."

They lift him up between them and place him gently down on the bed. He is a big man, the Boss, but they handle him as if he were as light as a wee birdie. "Good night, Mr. President," they say.

After the men have left, the president says, "Come here, pup."

He is sitting on the edge of his bed. I go to him and sniff at his slippers, at his thin ankles and spindly legs. They are as still and lifeless as the birdies in their glass cases.

"That's right, Fala," he says. "My legs are useless. Polio did that to me. I can walk, but only with ten pounds of metal braces on my legs. I'm telling you this because if you're to be my dog, it's very important that you obey my commands and come when you're called. Not because I'm the president of the United States. But because I cannot be chasing after you. My chasing days are behind me."

I jump up on his lap and give him a lick on the chin. *No worries, Boss. I'll stick to you like a burr to a Highlander's kilt.*

"Good dog," he says, stroking my back. "Let's both turn in. Tomorrow, we'll see how you behave yourself on your first picnic."

I jump down, crawl under his bed, and fall dead asleep.

The flag is still snapping over the front door when Prettyman wheels the Boss outside late the next morning. A long line of automobiles stands in the drive. For hours, everyone in the house has been preparing for the picnic. There are cars for picnickers and an entire car just to carry the food. Three people are already sitting in the backseat of the first car. The door is open, so I leap up into the front seat and get comfortable.

The Boss laughs as he settles in next to me. "You're going to have to let me drive this time, Fala. I know the way. Daisy, you'd better ride up front with us and keep an eye on this furry scamp."

I have not seen Miss Daisy since she left us in the Boss's study. I am so excited that I scramble into her lap and lick her face. *Long time no see!*

She pushes my muzzle away gently. "Have you been behaving yourself, Big Boy?" she asks.

"Fala," the Boss says.

"Ah!" Miss Daisy says with a shrewd nod. "How do you feel about being called Fala?" she asks me.

I whine. Truth to tell, I am a wee bit bamboozled. One day I am Big Boy. The next day I am Fala. What will I be tomorrow? Bonnie Prince Charlie?

Miss Daisy whispers to me as the Boss starts up the engine, "You're going to be a fine First Dog."

There is a gizmo rigged on the wheel. The Boss can make the car go without using his legs and feet. As he steers up the long drive, he points out trees to the passengers in the backseat. He knows the name of each tree and when it was planted and by which of his ancestors or neighbors. First birds and now trees. It seems the Boss and I have interests in common.

In the town nearby, he shows off the schoolhouse, which the Roosevelt family helped build, and St. James's, a lovely wee church with a boneyard in the back where his daddy is buried.

"I'm never happier and more carefree than when I'm here in the Hudson Valley," he says.

Once we get out on the paved roads, the Boss pulls out all the stops. There I am, standing on Miss Daisy's lap with my head hanging out the side of the automobile, tasting the fresh air and enjoying my wee bit of Dog Heaven. By the time the Boss stops the car, my fur is all swept away from my face. Daisy ruffles it back in place.

Ahead of us, barring passage, is a wooden blockade. Two men from the automobile behind us get out and move it.

"These gentlemen from the Secret Service come in mighty handy at times," the Boss says with a twinkle in his eye. "That's Mike Reilly and Dewey Long, Fala. They follow me everywhere, not unlike a pair of faithful hounds."

They do not look like hounds to me. They look like great burly toughs.

We drive up to the crest of a hill, where there is an old apple tree and a view of the river slithering along between its banks like a long snake. The automobiles stop, and everyone piles out. They get busy unpacking the baskets of food and loading up the plates. The smell of fried chicken makes my lips twitch. The Boss is lowered onto a blanket on the grass. He gets comfortable and holds out his

hand for a big drumstick. Parking myself in front of him, I stare at it with the full force of my personality. In other words, I beg.

"Knock it off," Miss Daisy scolds. "Ignore him, Mr. President. He's giving you the Treatment."

But the Boss says, "That's all right. He's just like Mrs. Roosevelt. He already knows I'm a soft touch." He peels off some skin and tosses it to me.

The picnickers lounge on their blankets and take turns sitting next to the Boss. After scouring the ground for dropped food, I amble off. I run into a few chipmunks and a band of sneering catbirds. A snooty little skunk sashays past me, and I give her a wide berth. I know these picnickers will be cross if I come back from my ramble stinking of skunk.

By the time I return, the sun hangs low over the distant mountains. A hush has fallen over the beasties, the birdies, the bugs, and even the people. In the shade of some bushes, one of the Boss's guests lies on his back with his hat over his head. He makes a strange rumbling noise. Och! Whatever is the matter with the man? I sniff at his shoes. I work my way up his body to his head and poke my nose under his hat. Suddenly, the snuffling turns into a loud yelp as he leaps to his feet.

"WHAT WAS THAT?" he shouts. He dances around, fingers madly brushing at his face.

Och, what have I done now? I fear I have made a proper mess of my first picnic.

Everyone bursts out laughing. Are they laughing at the yelping fellow or at me?

The Boss says, "That was Fala's cold nose you felt, Wallace! Wait'll the boys in the pressroom hear that a little dog nearly frightened the pants off the secretary of agriculture!"

Secretary Wallace grunts. He brushes the grass off his trousers and plops his hat on his head. "Nosy little pooch."

"Don't blame Fala," the Boss says. "That was his way of telling us that it's time to pack up and head for home—which was my thought exactly!"

I have passed the test. I am in!

THE FIRST DOG

Before I can move in with the Boss, Miss Daisy
must take me down to New York City. Onto those
crowded and noisy streets, yours truly goes forth
four times a day to walk at the end of a long leather
leash. I get used to the stink of the automobiles
and buses and streetcars, and to the ruckus of their
honking horns and backfiring tailpipes. I learn not
to pull too hard on the leash when I spy a squirrel or bird. I also learn not to let the leash get all

tangled up in my legs or around lampposts. But most important, I learn to do my business outside and to never, *ever* do it indoors.

If Miss Daisy has said it to me once, she has said it a thousand times: "There will be no dog doo in this president's White House if I can help it."

A few days after I have mastered leash training, a most remarkable incident occurs. I am stretched out, sunning myself on the window seat of Miss Daisy's bedroom, with one eye on a fat pigeon. Suddenly, I hear the Boss's voice in the next room.

I jump down and search for him. I look everywhere. It is the strangest thing, I tell you. I can hear the Boss's voice, but I cannot smell him. And there is nary a wheelchair in sight. There is only Miss Daisy huddled next to the big wooden box that sometimes makes music. And lo and behold, what is this I hear? Today, instead of music, the Boss's voice comes crackling and hissing out of the box.

Cocking my head, I growl.

I paw at Miss Daisy's foot. If this is the Boss's voice, where is the Boss? Och, say he is not trapped inside the box!

Daisy smiles. "That's your master, Fala, talking on the radio. He's far away in Virginia, at Arlington National Cemetery. He's making an Armistice Day address to the soldiers and sailors who fought in the last war. It's a wonderful speech. Let's listen."

Fala is no judge of speeches. But the sound of his voice is as sweet as Highland bagpipes to a Scotsman's ears. The Boss is saying:

"And so America is proud of its share in maintaining the era of democracy in that war in which we took part. America is proud of you who served—and ever will be proud. I, for one, do not believe that the era of democracy in human affairs can or ever will be snuffed out in our lifetime. I, for one, do not believe that mere force will be successful in sterilizing the seeds which have taken such firm root as a harbinger of better lives for mankind. I, for one, do not believe that the world will revert either to a modern form of ancient slavery or to controls vested in modern feudalism or modern emperors or modern dictators or modern oligarchs in these days. I, for one, do believe that the very people under their iron heels will, themselves, rebel."

The crowd listening to him breaks out in loud cheers. I bark, *You tell them, Boss!*

And then Miss Daisy flicks a button, and the Boss's voice is gone. I give her a good hard look.

She leans back with a deep sigh. "I hope he's right, Fala, because if those folks over in Europe don't get themselves out of the fix they're in,

America will go to war to help them."

War? I drop my nose onto my paws and stare up at her, worried. I like not the sound of this word.

We ride the train, Miss Daisy and I, down to Washington. Not only does it stink like motor oil and roar like the Loch Ness monster herself, but I have to sit in the back with the suitcases. Och! And as if all this weren't bad enough, Miss Daisy puts a leather muzzle on me. A porter, a Skinny Malinky Longlegs of a fellow, stops and stares down at me with a look of pity in his eye.

"You don't look very fierce to me," says he.

And do you know what that dear lad does? He takes off my muzzle. He frees Fala! I give him a good wet lick of thanks. When Miss Daisy comes to get me at the end of the trip, the look on her face is priceless!

Her eyes dart around, then settle on me. "Did

you take that muzzle off yourself?" she whispers.

I just stare at her and pant, *Och, lassie, that would be telling.*

From the train station, Miss Daisy tells a taxi-cab driver to take us to the White House.

White *House,* you say? The place ought to be called the White *Palace.* My chest puffs up. 'Tis a suitable residence, indeed, for a huge and powerful dog. Fala prepares himself for his grand entrance.

But Miss Daisy ruins it all by grabbing me up in her arms. She picks me up and carries me inside like a mere pup. Down a long hallway she walks. Everywhere I look, there are doors! Room after room! People come pouring out of them. So very many. Finally, a door opens up before us into an oval-shaped room. And there behind a grand desk, sitting in his wheelchair, is the man himself.

"Mr. President, I hope you are well. I've brought

you an early Christmas gift," Miss Daisy says.

I leap out of her arms, bolt across the room, and jump straight into his lap.

"There's my Fala!" the Boss says, laughing and scratching my head.

"He might be a bit overwhelmed by his new surroundings," Miss Daisy says. "Give him time."

"He doesn't look overwhelmed to me," says the Boss. "He looks ready to take on the House and Senate both. You never imagined you'd be master of such a mansion, did you, boy? Me neither. But here we are, all the same, and we're going to make the best of it. Do we have a deal?"

To clinch our deal, the Boss gives me a present. It is a smart-looking black leather collar. Riveted to the side of it is a fine silver plate with four words engraved in it. The Boss reads them aloud to me as he fastens the collar around my neck.

"FALA, THE WHITE HOUSE."

Naturally, they give me the run of the place. I smell the Boss's mate here, too, as I did up in Hyde Park. But I do not see her here, either. Could she still be traveling?

There is plenty for a dog to do here. I go dashing through the halls, using the Treatment on everyone I meet.

Spare a wee bite to eat?

You would be surprised at how many people carry dog treats in their pockets. Mrs. Nesbitt, the housekeeper, gives me scraps from the kitchen. And on top of all this, there are the bowls of food I get twice a day. I eat so much that my belly swells something fierce. By the fourth night, I lie around, too bloated and miserable to do anything but belch and groan.

I am not well! I need a doctor!

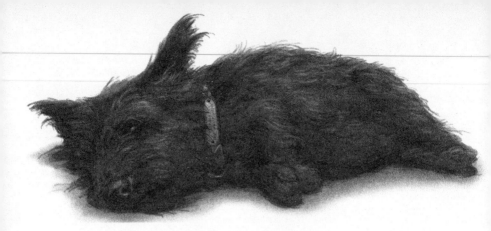

The Boss finally gets the message.

The next day, Mike Reilly takes me for a ride in his automobile. Too sick to enjoy Dog Heaven, I lie on the seat with my head drooping and listen to Mike grumble. "I signed on to protect the president, not his little dog."

I belch.

"Excuse you, buddy," says Mike.

I fear there is no excusing the sorry likes of Fala this day.

Mike takes me to the animal hospital. Some of the animals look even worse off than I do.

Mike says to the lady behind the desk, "This

here is the president's dog, and he's real sick."

Everyone in the room starts buzzing.

"Imagine, Franklin Roosevelt's own dog in the same room with us!" a woman whispers to her Siamese cat.

"See that, Fifi?" a man says to his poodle. "That there's the First Dog."

"The vet will see you next," the nurse tells Mike.

No fair cutting in line, says a disgruntled collie dog.

Sorry, Needlenose, I tell him. *This is a national emergency.*

The doctor takes me from Mike and puts me on a table. He pokes me and prods me and peers at me and finally says, "I think he'll live. But you might try not feeding him so much."

I could have told the man that! Och. Perhaps

I should get a white coat and become a doctor myself. Dr. Fala—it has a fine ring to it, does it not?

The doctor gives me some vile-tasting slime to soothe the ache in my belly.

Back at the White House, the Boss lets everyone know that no one—but no one—except the president himself gets to feed Fala from now on.

As a rule, I sleep under the Boss's bed. There, I feel safe from the tall, dark portraits on the walls frowning down at me. They seem to say, "So what's a silly wee beastie like you doing in a very important place like this?"

The Boss works in bed well into the night. I drift off to sleep to the sound of papers rustling. Early in the morning, before the Boss is awake, George, one of the Boss's valets, cracks open the door and whispers, "Come, Fala! Time to go out."

But I am reluctant to leave the Boss lying here sleeping and unprotected. Each morning, it takes me a little longer to come out from beneath the bed. Finally, I just lie there and dare the man to crawl across the rug and remove me by force from my post. George has no intention of doing such a thing. He has other ideas.

Before bedtime one night, he attaches a string that runs from my collar to the doorknob. Oh, he's a wily one, is our Georgie. He thinks that when he opens the door in the morning, he will be able to reel me in. But in the wee hours, I creep out from beneath the bed and go hunting dust bunnies. When George opens the door at dawn, he finds Fala trapped beneath a chair, hemmed in by a terrible tangle of string. I am even less pleased with this state of affairs than George.

So now, when he opens the door in the mornings, I scramble forth, bright-eyed and bushy-tailed, and go with him. I'll not tangle with string again anytime soon.

When I return from my morning walk, the Boss is usually sitting up in bed with his breakfast tray, eating scrambled eggs and bacon. There is always a nice big biscuit by his plate waiting for me. The Boss never feeds me without first asking me to do at least one trick. Sometimes, even after I have done the trick, the Boss will hang on to one end of the biscuit, as if he would like to keep it for himself.

I growl, *Hoot, man. Give me the blasted biscuit!*

Och, but he is a stubborn one. The Boss will not let go.

I growl louder, *I earned this biscuit! You owe me. Now pay up!*

Finally, laughing, he lets me have it. In a huff, I carry the biscuit to the middle of the rug and crunch it to bits. Some people have a very peculiar sense of humor, if you ask me.

By midmorning, the president is dressed and ready to go to work running the country. We ride the elevator down from the family floor to the offices below. A wee bell jingles, letting everyone know, "Look lively! The president is coming!"

"Good morning, Mr. President," they say. A few even say, "Good morning, Fala!"

Day after day, I am the proud head of the presidential parade, five steps ahead of the Boss in his wheelchair. Prettyman pushes. At his heels march the Secret Service guys, carrying wire baskets full of the papers the Boss has been working on. Usually, we go into the Oval Room. Sometimes we enter the pressroom for what's called a press conference. There, reporters fire questions at the Boss and the Boss answers them. I venture to say that the man is as good at answering questions as Fala is at performing tricks.

I do not follow the man everywhere, mind you. A few places are, for some reason, off-limits to Fala. When the Boss goes into the Cabinet Room for staff meetings, for instance, I am not to follow him. At first, I sulk. To cheer me up, Prettyman lets me out on the south lawn to play until the meeting is over. Afterward, I go rushing headlong into the Oval Room, bounce up onto the couch, and bury my head in a pillow and shake it.

This is Fala's way of saying, *Och. But it's good to be back! Did you miss me?*

And miss me they do. People cheer at the sight of me. Sometimes I run out and run in again, doing a repeat performance just to hear another round of cheers. Och! How I love the cheers.

Later, at teatime, I show off my best company manners. If visitors ignore me, I curl up in a corner and sleep. When the Boss's doctor, Admiral McIntire, comes to visit, I sidle up to him, put my head down on the floor sideways, and turn over on my back. The admiral rubs my stomach. He is a man after my own heart.

And whenever things get too quiet in the Oval Room, I Run Wild. This is when I make a mad dash around the room, under chairs and tables, out into the hall, and back in again. The Boss lunges toward me, trying to nab me. This only makes me pour on the speed. A furry black streak, I bank off the walls, ruck up the rugs, and leave a path of scattered knickknacks in my wake. Finally, I collapse in the middle of the floor and bask in the applause.

On quiet afternoons I follow the Boss down to

the basement swimming pool. I never go in. Fala is no water dog. I run along the edge and bark encouragement to the Boss as his powerful arms and chest plow through the water.

One day, I am looking out the Boss's window when I see a truck pull up, carrying a huge pine tree. I watch as men unload the tree and set it up on the south lawn. Next, they drag a bunch of smaller trees into the White House. Are all these trees for me? Tully may be reading my mind when she says, "Don't get any ideas about lifting your leg, Fala. These are *Christmas* trees. And they do not need watering by a little dog."

They set up the Christmas trees in pots all over the mansion and hang them with lights and shining balls. The place smells as sweet as all outdoors. I keep hoping they'll bring in some squirrels to go with the trees, but no such luck for Fala.

A few days after this, the Boss's mate finally makes an appearance. She comes to the name Eleanor, and she has presents and stories from her travels. I run up to her.

Welcome home, grand lass! I say to her.

She smiles down at me and says, "So you're Fala. I've heard all about you, young man."

I wag my wee tail and look up at her. *Is one of those presents for Fala?*

"I would give you a treat," she whispers, "only Franklin has told me, 'Eleanor! Don't feed Fala. He only takes food from me.' Is this true, Fala?"

I grin up at her. *Maybe he'll let you feed me if you are very good.*

Not long after she arrives, Eleanor sets loose a whole gaggle of little shavers. They tear up and down the halls, their happy voices ringing. And when they tire of dancing around the trees, they

turn to me. They chase me down and tickle my belly. Some of them try to pull my tail, but I am ever the gentleman. Being polite to grabby little children is exhausting work!

That night, family and staff gather around the tree in the Oval Room. The Boss reads aloud from a book called *A Christmas Carol.* I stretch out before the fireplace on a rug made of a real lion's skin from the far-off land of Ethiopia.

I fall asleep but wake up just in time to see the Boss handing out colorful packages. Inside the packages are shiny doodads called key rings. Diana, Harry Hopkins's daughter, runs up and jingles one of them in my face.

"See this, Fala?" the lassie says, pointing. "That's you."

Sure enough, on the key ring is a wee portrait of yours truly, Fala! Och! It touches my heart.

FALA'S FIRST CHRISTMAS

I wake up the next morning to the Boss's two-year-old grandson and Diana bouncing on the Boss's bed.

"Wake up, Papa! It's Christmas!" they cry. Other shavers come tumbling through the door.

Eleanor follows them in with her arms full of lumpy stockings. She hands one to the Boss and one to each child. She saves the last for me.

I wag my tail, peering up at her through my

fur. *For me? Really? Och, lass! You shouldn't have.*

"Merry Christmas, Fala!" she says with a big smile.

I take the stocking in my mouth and whip it back and forth until the presents inside fall out. Then I tear through the wrapping paper with my teeth. What's this? A brand-new rubber bone! I am so excited, I leap up and do every trick I know. I speak, but this time I do not say *please.* I say,

A blithe Yule and a good New Year to everyone!

"Look!" Diana laughs and points at me. "Fala's giving us a special Christmas-morning treat."

"Somebody had better take that puppy out for a walk soon, or he's going to give us another *kind* of Christmas treat," says the Boss with a grin.

Everyone laughs. Everyone is happy. Och, if we could only stay as happy as we are this day. But something in my Scots bones tells me that dark days lie ahead.

Before I go outside to do my business, I watch Eleanor open the gifts in her own stocking. What have we here? It is a wee Fala dog!

She sets the wee Fala on the rug and looks up at the Boss with a tender smile. "Is this from you, Franklin?" she asks.

"It's from Santa Claus!" the kids cry.

I circle in and sniff at it. It does not smell like

Dog to me. I shove it. It falls over on its side. What kind of dog is this? I am just about to give it a good bite when Eleanor snatches it away from me. "That's *my* Fala," she says. "You have your own toys."

Since coming to live here, I have learned this about Eleanor. Because it pains the Boss to travel distances, Eleanor goes all around, meeting with people and talking to them about what they believe in and want from their government. Then she comes back and reports in to the Boss. People say that, in this way, she and the Boss practically share the job of president. As far as I am concerned, the lass deserves to have her own Fala—even if it is nowhere near as smart or lively or charming as the real thing.

On a crisp day in January, the White House is all a-bustle. The Boss has put on a fancy suit and his leg braces, a dark coat, and a tall, shiny hat. A car pulls up in front of the White House. The top is down. The next time someone opens the door, I dash outside and jump into the backseat. If the Boss is going places, I am going with him.

After a while, the Boss comes out, and they lift him into the backseat next to me.

Where to, Boss? I want to know, my tongue hanging out eagerly.

"Sorry, Fala," the Boss says.

Surely the man is pulling my wee furry leg.

The next thing I know, some great hulking brute of a fellow reaches in and lifts me out of the car. "I hate to do this to you, little guy," he says. "But Senator Barkley and the Speaker of the House of Representatives need to get in there."

Then two men wearing black overcoats and tall, shiny hats squeeze into my place next to the

Boss. I growl, *See here, what is the meaning of this?*

As I later learn, today is Inauguration Day. The Boss is going over to the Capitol to get sworn in for a third term. The Capitol is off-limits for Fala.

A few days later, the Boss is hard at work on a new speech. He calls it his Annual Message to Congress. It must be a very important speech, because Harry Hopkins and Professor Sam and Robert Sherwood, another speechwriter, come to his study every day to work with him on it.

The Boss's desk chair is different from the one with two big wheels. This one has a tiny wheel on each leg. It rolls and swivels and dips and tips. Whenever the Boss is thinking hard, he tilts the chair way back and stares at the ceiling.

According to what I gather from my place beneath the desk, things are not going well across the sea in a place called Europe. A big, bad German bully by the name of Adolf Hitler is marching all over people. Hitler is a Nazi. Every time I hear this word, I shiver in my skin. The word sounds like oil sizzling on a hot stove. Norway, Denmark, Poland, France—many countries have already fallen beneath the boots of Nazis. The Nazis are now dropping bombs on the island nation known as Great Britain. Some of the British are huddling in bomb shelters, while others battle to fend off the Nazis.

No matter how bad it looks for the British, the people of America do not wish to go to war to help them. That is because most Americans today are what is called isolationist. They do not want America to get pulled into a war that has naught to do with them. But the Boss thinks of the British as America's cousins. He knows they need us. He wants to convince people that America has to make weapons and ships and planes to send to the

British. He thinks that winning this war is as important to America as it is to Britain. If the British lose to the Nazis, America might be their next target. The way he sees it, our own freedom is at stake.

After the Boss has tipped back in his chair for so long that I think he may have fallen asleep, he tips forward again and starts to speak.

Harry's pen starts scratching away on his pad. He copies down the Boss's words, and these will be the same words he will say to Congress a few days later.

I hear them on the radio in the Boss's bedroom:

"We look forward to a world based on four essential human freedoms.

"The first is freedom of speech and expression—everywhere in the world.

"The second is freedom of every person to

worship God in his own way—everywhere in the world.

"The third is freedom from want—which, translated into world terms, means economic understandings which will secure to every nation everywhere a healthy peacetime life for its inhabitants—everywhere in the world.

"The fourth is freedom from fear—which, translated into world terms, means a world-wide reduction of armaments to such a point and in such a thorough fashion that no nation will be in a position to commit an act of physical aggression against any neighbor—anywhere in the world."

In response to the Boss's urging, the weapons factories dust off their machinery and crank up. They turn out planes and tanks and guns for our cousins across the sea.

In these early days of spring, as the rumblings of war grow louder, everyone is far too busy to pay me much mind. Most afternoons, while the Boss meets with important leaders, I run free on the White House lawn.

There is this one squirrel I have my eye on. Och, and a sneakier little gink you never beheld! He stands on the grass right in front of me, nattering and chattering away: *You can't catch me!*

Care to see me try? I say. And off Fala goes. Up the squirrel leaps onto the iron fence and scampers onto the busy sidewalk.

This gets Fala to thinking about the great big world that lies beyond the iron fence. What a perfectly dandy place for a wee ramble! So I nose around and pretty soon come upon a spot beneath the fence where the earth has worn away. I get down on my belly and squeeze and squirm until I

slip underneath. And suddenly, Fala is free! I shake myself out and head off down the broad, busy avenue, like the Dog of the World that I am!

I trot along, sniffing and lifting my leg hither and yon, until I come upon a long line of lads and lasses standing on the sidewalk. I join them and, before long, the line begins to move.

Just as I am preparing to follow these folks inside, someone swoops down and grabs me.

THE DOG WHO OWNS A PRESIDENT

The fellow who has me in his clutches wears a hat with a shiny visor. My nose twitches at the sweet smell of him. Hot buttered corn! I lick his chin. He wipes it with the back of his white glove.

"Quit that," says he. He is trying hard not to smile. Putting a stern frown on his face, he says, "No dogs allowed in the movie theater, Rover."

Then he takes one look at my tag and whistles long and low. "Well, I'll be . . . !" he says. "You're

Fala, the president's dog! We'd better get you home."

He carries me down the street and right up to the White House guard. "Look who I found wandering around on the streets by himself," he says.

The guard's eyes bug. "Come with me, sir. He'll want to thank you personally."

My new friend sets me down on the floor of the Oval Room. He gazes around, all agog. (The Oval Room has that effect on people.) When I get a good look at the Boss's face, I hang my head.

"Where did you find him, son?" the Boss asks in a stern voice.

The man laughs uneasily. "He must be a Charlie Chaplin fan, Mr. President. We're showing *The Great Dictator* in the theater down the block. On the other hand, maybe he was there to see the newsreel of your inauguration, Mr. President."

Suddenly, the Boss throws back his head and

roars with laughter. "That's my Fala!" he cries. "I can see we're going to have to build a pen."

Alas! Fala's brief life as a Dog of the World is over.

The Boss is in a jolly good mood these days. The factories are humming. For the first time in a long time, people are working and taking home paychecks to feed their families. It looks like this Depression business is finally over. The American people have also begun to take notice of their cousins across the sea. They make packages to send to them. The packages contain food and clothes and blankets and toys for the kids. They are called Bundles for Britain.

Now, it so happens that there are many dog lovers among these generous American people. Someone has the brilliant idea to reward these dog lovers for their patriotism. Owners who put together bundles get a special tag for their dogs. It says *Barkers for Britain.* And guess who gets the number one tag?

Reporters and photographers swarm all over the south lawn. Usually, they are here to see President Roosevelt, but today, they have come to see me sworn in as president of Barkers for Britain. Something happens to me when the flashbulbs start to pop and crackle all around. I do my tricks. I smile. I pose. The photographers love me. And, what is more, I love them. I have always lapped up attention, but these lads and lasses really bring out the ham in me. The more I ham it up, the more pictures they snap, the more flashbulbs explode. It is better than a press conference. It is a press party presided over by yours truly: the Life of the Party. The pictures show up in newspapers across the country. When the Boss sees them, he is tickled pink.

Naturally, the fan mail begins to pour in. Tully reads the letters aloud to me. More photographers come and snap photos of me standing next to my sacks of mail. If I do say so myself, there is one excellent shot of me with my paws on the edge of a chair, looking at one of my letters. Not long after that, the Boss gets a letter from a bunch of schoolkids. Chuckling, he reads it aloud to everyone who visits the White House. It goes like this:

Dear Mr. Roosevelt:
We saw Fala's picture
in our Weekly Reader.
Did a dog write to Fala?
How can a dog write a letter?
Can a dog really read?
We hope your cold is better.
We have a very nice school.

Lord love them! What are they teaching kids these days? Everyone knows that dogs know naught of reading or writing. We have *humans* to do that for us! When the bags of mail begin to pile up, they get me my own personal secretary. Just like Tully and the Boss, she and I work together as a team. She types up the responses, and I add my signature.

It looks like this:

THE WHITE HOUSE
WASHINGTON

Dear Suzy:

I am very busy here at the White House, chasing squirrels and helping the president. But I am never too busy to answer nice letters like the one I got from you.

I even get a few letters from dogs whose masters have written for them. This one is my favorite:

```
To Fala
The dog who owns a president

Dear Fala:
You are indeed a fine fellow to
take on the presidency of the
Barkers for Britain League,
and I am writing to ask you if
you will allow me to join it.
I would indeed be very, very
proud to wear your badge. . . .
Anyhow, here's a wag of the
tail to a real pal,

(signed)
Aberdeen terrier, Beau
```

And have I told you how much a dog learns lying underneath his boss's desk and bed? I learn that the war in Europe is spreading at an alarming rate. When the Nazis fail to beat the British, they turn on a place called the Soviet Union, otherwise known as Russia. The Boss tells his aides that we have no choice but to help the Russians now that they, too, are under attack. American factories step up their already brisk pace to turn out even more weapons for the Russians.

Meanwhile, the Nazis are getting help of their own from the Empire of Japan. Up until now, America has been on friendly terms with the Japanese, selling them steel and oil. This must stop now, the Boss decides, slapping his desk. To sell the Japanese oil to run ships and planes will only help the Nazis. This decision does not come lightly to the Boss. The Japanese will be furious with America. The bedsprings over my head squeak as the Boss tosses and turns, night after night, fretting over his decision to cut off the Japanese.

Whenever all the troubles of the world begin to weigh on him, the Boss takes to the sea. Something in the salty air and the vast gray stretches of water frees him. "Fala," he says to me, "if I hadn't been president, I would have been a seafaring man."

That spring we go on a fishing trip down south with some lucky members of his staff. The Boss has a special chair on the boat that he sits in to fish. I do not fish, but there is plenty for Fala to do, and most of it, I tell you, is with my nose. Och, the scents at sea! Fish and starfish, seaweed and seagulls, and wonderful big pails of worms and stinking, slimy fish guts. I sit up on deck and try to catch the gulls when they swoop down to pick at the guts. Meanwhile, the Boss sits in the aft with his fishing rod propped up and his hook baited. He hauls in one wriggling fish after another. What strange creatures these fishies are!

One day, the fish are biting fast and furious. Everyone who tosses a hook in the water—Harry,

Sam, Robert Sherwood, even each of the Secret Service guys—reels in a fish. There is a great pile of them on deck, their silver scales flashing in the sunlight. They flip and flop. It is as if they believe that by flipping and flopping hard enough, they might land themselves back in the sea.

At first, all this fishy flopping gets my goat. I snap and bark at them. *Settle down! Fala wishes you fishies to be still now!*

But they pay no attention to me. That is when I say to myself, *Fala, if you cannot lick them, why not join them?*

I start flip-flopping like the fishies. I somersault, tumbling head over heels, until I nearly flip overboard. When the people see me, they break out laughing. And nothing makes Fala happier than getting a good laugh.

For days after that, whenever there is a dull

moment or a lull in the conversation, I do my new trick. In time, the laughs begin to fade. How can I keep the laughs going? Perhaps I need to flip higher or flop faster? Finally, I flip so high I flop onto my furry bahookie.

Professor Sam takes me aside and says, "Fala, the fish trick? It's starting to get a little old. I think it's time you gave it up."

Och, well. I can take a hint. No more flip-flops for Fala.

Summer of '41 comes on hot and humid. Some nights, it gets so roasty-toasty I have to crawl out from beneath the Boss's bed and sleep stretched out on the cool marble floor. At the beginning of August, the Boss tells reporters we are getting out of town. We are taking a cruise on the USS *Potomac* up to Maine "to get some cool nights." No one knows—not Tully, not even Eleanor—that we are really going on a Secret Mission. But I'll tell you who does know: the Boss's two grown lads, Elliott and Franklin, Jr., because they are coming with us. This tells me that wherever we are going, the Boss is going to be doing some walking. The Boss fancies leaning on his lads when he walks.

We are two days out to sea when a huge navy cruiser comes alongside us. The USS *Augusta* is big enough to swallow the wee *Potomac.* I run back and forth on deck, barking, as the crew moves all our gear from the *Potomac* onto the *Augusta.* Then we board the *Augusta.*

The Boss seems happy and excited. Up the coast toward Canada we steam, escorted by a fleet of navy destroyers. I sit up on deck and give the hairy eyeball to these ships.

I know something is up on the day when the Boss gets out of his bunk and puts on a fancy suit. Suits are for land, not for boats and ships. He has also put on those leg braces of his. Today, the Boss is going to stand up and walk. Och! Walk on board a ship? Is he off his head?

On the bridge, the captain announces that the British ship HMS *Prince of Wales* is across the bay from us. We all watch as a launch boat departs from her port side and plows through the water toward us. Standing with the Boss are his lads, both dressed in their soldier uniforms.

The launch comes alongside. Our captain hails them. A military band strikes up a tune as a chubby little man with pink skin and a face like a bulldog comes aboard. Leaning heavily on Elliott and a cane, the Boss makes his way across the deck to meet the man. I fret. What if a big wave should come along, jostle the ship, and send the Boss sprawling onto his presidential bahookie? Mercifully, the sea remains calm. The chubby little man meets the Boss halfway. They clasp hands and smile at one another.

I breathe a huge sigh of relief.

"At last—we've gotten together," the Boss says.

Nodding, the other man replies, "We have."

The man gives the Boss an envelope. I later learn it is a letter from the king of England himself.

No one notices when I go up and sniff at the trouser leg of the chubby little man. He might look like a bulldog, but he smells like a cat.

The Man Who Smells Like a Cat

His name is Winston Churchill, this man who smells like a cat, and he is the prime minister of the British people. The Boss's little get-together with him is our Secret Mission. By the time their luncheon is over, they are fast friends, calling each other Winston and Franklin.

Whenever I go up to the Minister to say howdy-do, he gives me the brush-off. Is this because he is a Cat Person? Cat People can be funny about us dogs. Some of them are afraid of us. Others flat-out want naught to do with us. But maybe he has more important things on his mind than making friends with a wee black Scottie.

At dinner, the Minister and the Boss speak of their hopes and dreams. They both love the sea and studying the great naval battles of history. Finally, the Minister gets down to business after dinner. With a fat cigar clenched in his teeth, he tells the Boss that he needs big bomber planes, and lots of them. He wants to bomb the Nazis, make them go away, and never let them come back.

The next day, it is the Boss's turn to visit the Minister's ship. Once again, the Boss dons a suit and leg braces and prepares to brave the world at sea on his own two feet. This time, the captain brings our ship alongside the *Prince of Wales*. The British sailors toss a gangway between the two ships and make it fast. On Elliott's arm, the Boss walks across the wobbly gangway. People have tried to talk him into using the wheelchair today, but he will hear naught of it. Sometimes it is important for the president of the United States to stand on his own two feet, no matter how hard and painful and risky it might be.

The Minister greets him on the other side of the gangway. Still balancing on his lad's arm, the Boss walks with the Minister across the quarterdeck toward the chair that is meant for him.

The crew of the *Wales*—officers and sailors, all dressed in uniform—tall. I am thinking what a grand man the Boss is when someone nearby pipes up:

The Minister says your president is a very great man, but I don't see it myself.

My head snaps around. Who said that? Who

dares to speak this way about the Boss?

A black cat sits nearby, licking his paw.

What did you say? I bear down upon him.

The cat shakes out his paw and starts to clean his chest with his tongue. He stops long enough to comment, *All I'm saying is that the bloke moves like a weakling.*

His legs might not be very strong, but his heart and mind are as stout as those of any man alive.

He pauses in his licking. *Really? Is he brave enough to fight a war, the way my people have been doing for two years with no help from you Yanks?*

Believe me, he would march into battle tomorrow. But his people are isolationists. They want no direct involvement in your European war.

Then he should make them. What good is a leader if he can't make his people do his bidding?

It doesn't work that way in America. The people's

will rules. It's called democracy, you wee furry flea-brain.

No need to take it personal. Say, what's your name?

Murray the Outlaw of Falahill.

Really? Tell me you actually come to that blinking ridiculous name?

Not really, no. I come to Fala.

That's better. Call me Blacky. I'm the ship's cat.

I have no great fondness for cats. But something about this one is beginning to grow on me. The way he speaks his mind. The way he smells like the sea. And then there is his splendid black coat.

We watch, Blacky and I, as the sailors who have come over from our ship join the ones from Great Britain. They stand together, shoulder to shoulder, and raise their voices in song.

"O God, our help in ages past,
Our hope for years to come,
Our shelter from the stormy blast,
And our eternal home . . ."

Now I understand. This is a Sunday service, like the kind the Boss goes to at St. James's Church, up at Hyde Park. The cat and I lie down in the sun and doze while the ship's chaplain gives a sermon and leads the company in prayer. Afterward, they sing another hymn:

"Onward, Christian soldiers,
Marching as to war,
With the cross of Jesus
Going on before!

Christ, the royal Master,
Leads against the foe;
Forward into battle,
See his banners go!"

I look over at the Minister, sitting next to the Boss. He is wiping the tears from his eyes with a handkerchief.

Your Minister likes to act tough, I say to Blacky. *But I can see he is really a soft touch.*

True enough, Blacky says, *as most cat lovers are, deep down.*

After the Sunday service, the Minister shows the Boss around the ship. Blacky gives me my own tour. I get back just in time to join the Boss for Sunday dinner. The Minister is serving grouse, one of the tastier game birds. The Boss slips me a few morsels beneath the table. I growl with pleasure. *My compliments to the steward.*

When it comes time to leave, the Minister sees us off across the gangway.

Fala, I'd like to come and take a look around your ship, Blacky says.

You are welcome to do so, I say, happy to return the favor.

Blacky is just setting off after me when someone says, "Not so fast, Puss-Puss."

The Minister sweeps Blacky up in his arms. "Your place is on board this ship," he tells him.

Och, well! Perhaps some other time, I tell Blacky.

He is purring away as the Minister's chubby pink fingers stroke his silken coat.

Cheerio, Fala. It's been jolly nice meeting you, he says.

Likewise, I'm sure. Smooth sailing and good luck with your war.

WARM SPRINGS

After we return to the White House, the Boss and I listen to the Minister speaking on the radio to his people. Just as the Boss has his weekly Fireside Chats—when he speaks on the radio to the American people—the Minister likes to talk to the British. Today, he is telling them all about his secret meeting with the Boss.

"It symbolizes, in a form and manner which everyone can understand in every land and every clime, the deep underlying unities which stir and at decisive moments rule the English-speaking peoples throughout the world. Would it be presumptuous of me to say that it symbolizes something even more majestic—namely: the marshaling of the good forces of the world against the evil forces which are now so formidable and triumphant and which have cast their cruel spell over the whole of Europe and a large part of Asia?"

To listen to the Minister, you would think that America was raring to join Britain in the war.

But when reporters later ask the Boss, "Is America closer to war?" the Boss shakes his head.

He wants to help the Minister. I know he does. It is just that he still does not believe the American people feel as strongly about it as he does. And he does the people's bidding.

Besides worrying about the war, the Boss has

other problems. His mommy has up and died. While she and I never quite hit it off, I know that she loved her lad dearly. As he mourns her, so do I. I stay by his side, ready to cheer him up if cheering is called for. But there is no cheer for the Boss this day.

Long, long ago, BF (that is to say, Before Fala), when the Boss first got the disease that crippled him, he heard tell that the spring waters in a place called Warm Springs, Georgia, had cured a wee lad of polio. With high hopes, he spent many months in that place. He soaked himself in the healing waters. He exercised his lifeless legs and strengthened his shoulders and arms. Sadly, the waters did not cure him. But they did make him feel strong enough to return to public life. Eventually, he won the office of the presidency. Imagine, a man who has lost the power to use his legs, winning such an important race! Och, what a man! The strength and courage of him! It makes my Scottish heart sing.

The Boss has a special connection to Warm Springs—body, mind, and soul. He even bought a house near the healing waters. With the help of friends, he has turned the place into a big organization. It opens its doors to people with polio to come and soak in the waters. The organization is dedicated to soothing the suffering caused by polio, and to finding a cure for it. Every Thanksgiving, the Boss travels down to Warm Springs. Much of the staff goes there with us, including the Secret Service guys, Harry Hopkins, Professor Sam, Tully, and even Hackey, the White House telephone operator. People in Washington and around the world have to be able to reach the Boss at any time. Hackey is the only person he trusts to make sure all these important calls get through to him.

We sit down to Thanksgiving dinner. The cook brings out a big roast turkey. On this day, the Boss seems not to mind all the bits of meat and skin that are slipped to me beneath the table. This, truly, is something for Fala to be thankful for.

The next day, Hackey puts through a call to the Boss from the secretary of state. We can all hear Mr. Hull's voice through the telephone. The crisis with Japan is getting worse!

The Boss hangs up the telephone. I have never

seen him so rattled. Naturally, the Boss being nervous puts everyone else on edge. We all try to relax. The Boss sits for hours working on his stamp album, peering through a magnifying glass at his tiny treasures. The Army-Navy football game plays on the radio.

At dinner the Boss makes a little speech. Everyone puts down knives and forks to listen. He says in a voice that quavers with sadness, "It may be that next Thanksgiving these boys of the Military Academy and of the Naval Academy will be actually fighting for the defense of these American institutions of ours."

Later that night, Secretary Hull calls again. Afterward, the Boss claps his hands and tells us all to look lively. We have just arrived. But it seems we are packing up and heading back to Washington.

It is as if a dark storm is approaching.

INFAMY!

On a Sunday shortly after Thanksgiving, the Boss and Harry are having lunch in the Oval Room when the secretary of the navy calls. I watch the Boss's face turn from rosy to ashen. He hangs up.

"It's finally happened," he says in a whisper. "We're under attack from the Japanese at Pearl Harbor. We don't yet have the death count, but it's bound to be high."

Does the Boss look like the commander in chief

of the armed forces this day? Hardly. He is wearing his slippers and a sloppy old sweater. But there is no doubt in anyone's mind that he is alert and in charge. The nervousness is gone. He sits at his desk giving orders, signing messages, and talking on the telephone. He speaks to General Marshall about where to move the American troops. He speaks with Secretary Hull. Toward dinnertime, he sends for Tully.

"Sit down, Grace," he says to her.

I sit down, too, on the floor by his feet. Tully and I look to the Boss, eyes bright, ready.

The Boss says, "I'm going before Congress tomorrow. I'd like to dictate my message."

He begins: "Yesterday (comma) December 7 (comma) 1941 (dash) a day which will live in infamy (dash) the United States of America was suddenly and deliberately attacked by naval and air forces of the Empire of Japan (period, paragraph)." He continues without a single hesitation or stumble. Toward the close of the speech, he says, "I ask that the Congress declare that since the unprovoked and dastardly attack by Japan on Sunday (comma) December 7 (comma) a state of war has existed between the United States and the Japanese Empire (period, end)."

The next day, I listen to him on the radio making this speech.

For the Boss, for the staff, for reporters, for the American people, and for people around the world, the day the Japanese bombed Pearl Harbor will forever be known as the Day That Will Live in Infamy.

Everyone expects the Boss to send troops to the Pacific to get back at the Japanese. The Boss sends troops there, but he sends more to Europe. He wants to beat Hitler and the Nazis. That's where the trouble started and that's where he hopes to end it. The way he explains it to the people, in one of his Fireside Chats, is like this: "We are now in the midst of a war, not for conquest, not for vengeance, but for a world in which this nation, and all that this nation represents, will be safe for our children. We expect to eliminate the danger from Japan, but it would serve us ill if we accomplished that and found that the rest of the world was dominated by Hitler and Mussolini."

Two days later, as if they have been listening to the Boss on the radio, Hitler and his Italian ally, Mussolini, declare war on America. The Boss and Congress declare war right back.

If we were in up to our chins before, we are in up to our eyebrows now.

In the midst of all this excitement, guess who shows up for Christmas? Winston Churchill himself. The Boss drives to the airport to meet the old boy.

The next morning, on my way out to the south lawn, I make the rounds. I dash into one of the guest bedrooms and there he is, scowling with the cigar clenched in his teeth.

Long time no see! I give the Minister an eager little bark, expecting the usual snub in return.

"Well, little dog, I see they give you the run of the place, just like me," he says.

He reaches down and pats my head. Granted, it is in that clumsy way that Cat People touch dogs. But give the man credit for trying.

Something about having this fellow in the White House changes it. Maybe it is the smell of his cigar. Maybe it is the sight of him wandering the halls. Or maybe it's the sound of him, cane thumping, and yammering away to anyone who will listen! Och, but the man loves to run his mouth! He is one silver-tongued Englishman.

The Minister has brought cases of maps with him. This inspires the Boss to set up a Map Room. There, he has taped up the entire world on the walls, with little pins to show where all the armies are. The Boss and the Minister spend hours in the Map Room, moving those pins around.

The Boss holds a press conference. The gentlemen and ladies cram into the pressroom.

The Minister climbs up on a chair and waves to the crowd.

The reporters pelt him with questions. One of them asks, "Do you think the war is turning in our favor in the last month or so?"

The Minister says, "I can't describe the feelings

of relief with which I find Russia victorious, the United States and Great Britain standing side by side. It is incredible to anyone who has lived through the lonely months of 1940. It is incredible. Thank God."

"Mr. Minister, can you tell us when you think we may lick these boys?"

The Minister pauses. "If we manage it well," he says with a smile, "it will only take half as long as if we manage it badly."

Everyone laughs.

Later, another reporter asks, "Mr. Minister, have you any doubt of the ultimate victory?"

"I have no doubt whatever."

I look up at the Boss, at whose feet I sit. He is grinning from ear to ear. It is the same way he looks at me when I do tricks for guests.

On Christmas Eve, the Boss and the Minister

go out onto the south lawn and light up the big tree. The Boss tells the crowd that has gathered, "Our strongest weapon in this war is that conviction of the dignity and brotherhood of man which Christmas Day signifies—more than any other day or any other symbol."

The people burst into Christmas songs. When the singing stops, the Minister steps up to the microphone. If Santa Claus himself had come to speak to the people, he would not have pleased them half as much as the Minister did that evening.

"I spend this anniversary and festival far from my country, far from my family, yet I cannot truthfully say that I feel far from home. . . . Here, in the midst of war, raging and roaring over all the lands and seas, creeping nearer to our hearts and homes, here, amid all the tumult, we have tonight the peace of the spirit in each cottage home and in every generous heart. Therefore we may cast aside for this night at least the cares and dangers which beset us, and make for the children an evening of happiness in a world of storm. Here, then, for one night only, each home throughout the English-speaking world should be a brightly lighted island of happiness and peace. . . . Let the children have their night of fun and laughter. Let the gifts of Father Christmas delight their play. Let us grown-ups share to the full in their unstinted pleasures before we turn again to the stern task and the formidable years that lie before us, resolved that, by our sacrifice and daring, these same children shall not be robbed of their inheritance or denied their right to live in a free and decent world. And so, in God's mercy, a happy Christmas to you all."

And a blithe Yule to you, too, Mr. Minister!

HOLLYWOOD COMES TO FALA

In the summer of '42, the Minister comes to visit us at Hyde Park. The Boss and I meet him at the airport. We show the Minister all our favorite spots along the Hudson River. Every time the Boss races his automobile to the edge of one of the high bluffs overlooking the mighty river, the Minister grips the dashboard and gasps, "I trust our brake mechanism is in working order, Franklin."

The Boss laughs. He might be careful when it

comes to world affairs, but behind the wheel of an automobile, he is a wild man.

One afternoon, the Boss and the Minister sit in the study, talking about something called Tube Alloys. I have not the faintest idea what that means, until one of them says that the discovery of Tube Alloys by scientists will make possible the biggest and most deadly bomb ever known to humankind.

Och! Why are they even discussing such a thing? Are these lads off their heads?

It seems that German scientists are looking to make the very same bomb. A desperate race is going on. Whoever makes the bomb first will win the war. It is madness.

Afterward, we all pile into the Boss's automobile. He drives us up to a little stone cottage at the top of a rise. The Boss has built the cottage so he has a place to get away from the house, which is very crowded these days. He calls it Top Cottage.

Top Cottage is where we often bring small groups to have picnics and, much to my delight, roast hot dogs on an open fire. Miss Daisy is hostess this day. She serves the men refreshments and me a wee dram of broth. Much to my relief, there is no more talk about Tube Alloys.

During this visit, the Minister receives upsetting news. His armies have suffered a terrible defeat in North Africa. A Nazi general named Rommel has outsmarted the British. This, on top of the trouncing the British have taken in Singapore, has laid the Minister lower than I have ever seen the man.

The Boss rests a hand on the Minister's shoulder.

"What can we do to help?" he asks, not as one great leader to another, but as a true friend.

The Minister looks up at him and says, "Give

us as many Sherman tanks as you can spare."

The Boss not only ships those tanks, but sends soldiers as well. In November, the Allied armies, British and Americans united, invade North Africa and take it back from the Nazis. Thanks to American weapons and American soldiers—thanks to the Boss—the tide of battle has begun to shift.

You might be wondering what Fala, naught but a wee Scottie dog, can possibly do to help out with the war effort. Well, I do my modest part. It all started with a book Daisy wrote. It is called *The True Story of Fala*. The book has become a bestseller. I figure it gives people something cheerful to take their mind off the war. The Boss calls it morale boosting. It is so successful that a bunch of people in Hollywood, California, have decided to make it into a moving picture.

When I first get wind of this scheme, I jump for

joy. Is it possible that I, Fala, am going to become the next Rin Tin Tin? What dog wouldn't want to have his paw pressed into the damp cement of the Hollywood Walk of Fame? As it turns out, the reality is a tad less glamorous.

To begin with, alas, it is not one of those big, long moving pictures. It is what they call a short, a one-reeler. But the way those geniuses carry on, you would think we were filming *Gone with the*

Wind. They show up one day and take over the White House like an invading army. They block the hallways with their cameras and gizmos. They run wires every which way. And the lights! Och! They have enough spotlights with them to blind a whole cast of dogs. But I have grown up in the shadow of the Boss. The Boss lives in the glare of the spotlights. So it will take a lot more than bright lights to scare Fala.

What does put me off, however, is strangers yelling, "Cut!" and "Roll 'em!" every time I stop to scratch. Then there are the ridiculous, unreasonable demands.

"Bark, Fala."

"Dig up that bone, Fala."

"Run and stop on this mark, Fala."

"Smile, Fala."

When they look around for a squirrel I can chase, there are none to be had. The moviemakers have scared away all the squirrels. They send a runner to the zoo to borrow one. When they open the cage, they say, "Chase the squirrel, Fala!"

The squirrel just stands there, too terrified to move.

You're supposed to run, you wee gink, you, I tell him.

Off the squirrel goes like a shot. Off Fala goes

after him. The cameras roll. The moment is captured.

After that, they all run around trying to catch that squirrel so they can put him back in the cage and return him to the zoo. You never saw such commotion. And the sight of humans chasing a squirrel! Well, I have myself a fine chuckle over that one.

Then they ask the wee lass Diana to hunker down with me by the fireplace and gaze at one of my scrapbooks. What do I care about a bunch of paper and pictures?

Diana says to the cameraman, "If you put some bacon on the pages, I bet Fala will put his nose right where you want it."

Bacon! I am almost never allowed bacon. Off to the kitchen they go to beg Mrs. Nesbitt for some bacon. When they rub the bacon on the pages of my scrapbook, I fairly lick the pages clean. And another memorable moment is captured.

But just in case Fala fails to cooperate, they bring in a stunt double. Just like Fala, he is a black Scottie. Some staffers have mistaken him for me, but we look nothing alike. Oh, he is a handsome-enough laddie. But his fur is far too tidy. They have to mess it up to give him my rough-and-tumble good looks. And the sparkle in my eyes? His eyes are dim, I tell you. Unlike me, this dog does *not* have a huge and powerful personality. On the contrary, it is puny. He is about as much use to me as a wink to a blind horse. And, as it turns out, his services are not needed, thank you very much. Fala has the matter well in paw.

Let me not forget this Pete Smith fellow. His job is to pretend to speak in my voice. If Fala could talk like a man, Pete Smith would be the last man on earth he would want to sound like.

Things pick up in the last section of the movie, when the subject turns to war. Pete Smith says that even I—Fala, the First Dog—have been forced to make sacrifices for the war effort. I have given up my rubber balls and bones, because rubber is needed to make wheels for army vehicles. True, I have made my small sacrifices, just as the Boss has sacrificed some of his beloved Hyde Park trees for building warships. The film ends by showing the Boss in the Oval Room, pinning medals on war heroes. There are no stunt doubles in this scene. These heroes, like yours truly, are the real McCoy.

One day early in 1943, the Boss packs for a trip. I can tell he is not taking Fala with him.

He reaches down and rubs my shaggy head.

"I'm flying to Casablanca for a very big meeting with Winston and others. It's the first time any president has flown. I don't think you'd like it, Fala."

As it turns out, in the months ahead, I will fly and, in fact, grow to like shooting through the air like a hawk. Before I know it, the Boss and I are winging it all over the place. We fly up to Canada for a conference, across the country to inspect army bases, and down south to visit munitions factories. If you ask me, the Boss is getting a little carried away with this flying business. Flying is hard on his body! The man looks more exhausted with each passing day.

In August 1944, we sail to Alaska from Hawaii to visit a military base. We eat our meals with the soldiers in a great drafty Quonset hut. The highlight of the tour is a fishing trip to Kodiak

Island. How happy the Boss is with the huge fish he catches. But this harmless little fishing trip winds up causing him a big amount of trouble.

The Boss is running for his fourth term of office. No American president has ever served a fourth term. And the Republicans are fighting hard to prevent it from happening.

It is not as if the Boss even wants to serve for a fourth term. The man is tired. He wants to retire to Hyde Park and rest. But, bless him, as long as the war rages on, he feels the need to see his nation through to peacetime.

The Republicans set out to blacken the Boss's good name. This is how they do the deed. Our ship was briefly delayed, owing to the threat of bad weather. So the Republicans start the rumor that the delay was caused, not by Mother Nature, but by the Boss accidentally leaving Fala behind on Kodiak Island. At a cost of millions of dollars to the taxpayers, they claim, the Boss had to send a navy destroyer back to pick me up. Hoot, man! That's naught but pure Republican bunkum!

By September, the Fala Scandal is still going strong. Fed up, the Boss makes a campaign speech. As he comes to the end of it, I hear him speak my name. My ears perk up.

The Boss is saying: "These Republican leaders have not been content with attacks on me, or my wife, or on my sons. No, not content with that, they now include my little dog, Fala. Well, of course, I don't resent attacks, and my family doesn't resent attacks, but Fala does resent them. You know, Fala is Scotch, and being a Scottie, as soon as he learned that the Republican fiction writers in Congress and out had concocted a story that I had left him behind on the Aleutian Islands and had sent a destroyer back to find him—at a cost to the taxpayers of two or three, or eight or twenty, million dollars—his Scotch soul was furious. He has not been the same dog since. I am accustomed to hearing malicious falsehoods about myself— such as that old, worm-eaten chestnut that I have represented myself as indispensable. But I think I have a right to resent, to object to, libelous statements about my dog."

When it turns out that he wins the election for a fourth term, am I surprised? Och, no! Any man willing to leap to the defense of his dog is all right with the American people.

THE UNFINISHED PORTRAIT

In February, after the Boss's fourth inauguration, he travels again without me to a place in Europe called Yalta to meet with Prime Minister Churchill and with Stalin, the Soviet president. They are meeting to discuss how to bring about the final defeat of the Germans.

When the Boss comes back from his trip, I dance for joy. But the Boss can barely lift his hand to pat me. He looks so peely-wally! So sickly and frail! And the circles under his eyes! When he goes to make a speech to Congress, for the first time ever he sits in a chair instead of standing. The speech is excellent and the news from Yalta is good. But everyone is shocked at how poorly the Boss is looking.

When I learn we are going down to Warm Springs, a wave of sheer relief washes over my shaggy head. The healing waters of Georgia will put the Boss back in fine fettle. A group of us ride down on the train. His aide Bill Hassett comes, as do the Secret Service fellows. Also on board are Tully and Hackey and three eager lads from the press.

As tired as he is, the Boss tries to do a wee bit of work each day so he will not fall too far behind.

Madame Elizabeth Shoumatoff arrives to paint a new portrait of him. He poses for it wearing his wool navy cape.

I am napping, but I hear him say to Madame Shoumatoff, "We only have fifteen minutes."

I open one eye and see him reach up to touch the side of his head. "I have a terrific pain in the back of my head," he says. I close my eye and return to an uneasy sleep.

After a bit, I awake to see the Boss again put his hand to his head. Then he slumps backward.

Madame Shoumatoff lets out a small cry. I leap up, run over, and lick the Boss's hand. I like not the taste of it. Prettyman and another fellow run to the Boss's side. They lift him and carry him to the bedroom.

I follow and stand by the bed.

Everything is happening very quickly. I have to

move fast to avoid getting stepped on. Then, amid all the commotion, I hear the Boss's voice. I look at the frail body lying on the bed. The voice isn't coming from there. It is coming from somewhere else. It is in the very air, ringing all around me, just as clear as the bells of St. James's.

I have to go now, Fala, the voice says. *But we'll be together soon. You be a good dog in the meantime and obey Daisy.*

I dash outdoors and look around for the Boss.

I am befuddled. Where is he going? I lift my head and bark with all the power of my soul, my proud and furious Scottish soul.

"What's wrong with Fala?" I hear someone say.

"Dogs have a second sense about these things," someone answers.

A car comes speeding down the driveway. A door opens, and Admiral McIntire, the Boss's doctor, dashes into the house. Not long afterward, he comes out. "The president is dead," he says.

Hassett whispers, "Someone find the First Lady."

Some people cover their faces and sob. Others just sit and stare. A few run to the telephones and speak in fast, nervous voices. I stay outside and bark, hoping the Boss will hear me. Sometime later, when my throat is ragged, Daisy kneels beside me and weeps into my fur.

"Our dear president's gone. We're all alone now."

I turn and lick the tears from her face.

The press laddies start firing questions.

"What was the cause of death?" one of the lads asks Hassett.

"A massive cerebral hemorrhage."

"Had you seen the president today?"

"Yes, at noon. He signed some bills."

"Was he ill then, or in good spirits?"

"He seemed to be fine. He even joked."

"Who was with him when he was stricken?"

I was, I want to say. *I was with him, as I always am and always will be.*

The aide answers, "Madame Shoumatoff was there. She was working on the portrait."

"Did he have any warning of the attack, or know it was coming?"

"Madame Shoumatoff says that he had re-minded her, 'We only have fifteen minutes.' He collapsed exactly fifteen minutes later."

Sometime later, Eleanor arrives. The brave lass takes charge without shedding a single tear. After a while, she looks around and asks, "Where is Fala?"

I bark. *Over here!*

Miss Daisy says, "I have him. The president wanted me to take care of Fala if anything ever happened to him."

Eleanor's chin wobbles. For the first time, her eyes fill with tears. Could it be she wishes the Boss had asked her instead of Daisy?

I go home on the train with Miss Daisy. At her house, I lie on my belly and mope.

A few days later, James, one of the Boss's sons, shows up. He and Daisy speak. Eleanor wants me to live with her in Hyde Park, but she is too upset to ask Daisy herself. Much as I have always loved Miss Daisy, this news fills me with joy. Hyde Park is my forever home.

A week later, Daisy drives me there. *Perhaps,* I am thinking, *the Boss will be waiting for me at the house.*

But the Boss is not there. Instead, there is a huge crowd of friends and strangers milling about the rose garden. They hold flowers and hug each other. A military band plays music. Then some soldiers march stiffly into our midst. They line up and cock their rifles and fire at the sky. My eardrums are fit to burst. I commence to howling. They keep firing. I howl all the louder. Still, they fire. Daisy kneels down and tries to comfort me.

"He's mourning his master," she explains to the people around us.

I am just about to attack the nearest soldier

when they stop. My poor ears ring. The air is filled with the smoke and the smell of gunpowder.

The long day drags onward. There are cameras rolling and reporters taking notes. There are speeches and sermons and prayers. Finally, two lines of men, among them the Boss's sons, carry a long wooden box covered with a flag into the rose garden. They lower the box into a hole. Later, they fill in the hole with dirt and mark the spot with a big, shiny stone rectangle.

"That's where the president lies," Miss Daisy says.

I shoot her a sour look and growl, *The Boss is not lying beneath some piece of rock. The Boss is off at a conference. Anytime now he will be coming home.*

Eleanor and I begin our long wait. The years pass. Eleanor has no trouble keeping herself busy. She reads and she writes and she has friends come to visit. It is harder for Fala, so Daisy brings her new Scottie dog over to keep me company. Her name is Button, and you can bet that she is every bit as cute as one. With her, I sire a couple of pups, Little Peggie and Fala McFala, who become the dear companions of my later years. Together, we

ramble over the grounds. But I never ramble very far in case the Boss should decide to return.

People often come to visit the big stone rectangle in the rose garden. They lay wreaths and flowers on it and tell stories about the Boss.

Once, the gates swing open. A big black automobile comes crunching down the drive, followed by Secret Service cars. My heart leaps. *Boss? Is that you?*

I spring to my feet and run to meet the automobile. But it is General Eisenhower. He has come to lay a wreath on the stone rectangle in the rose garden. I slink away with my ears drooping.

I begin to spend more time lying around stretched out on my belly. I am careful to park myself near the dining room, where I can keep an eye on the front door. When the Boss comes, I will jump up and greet him and never let him out of my sight again. Wherever he wants to go, I will go with him. On a boat trip down south to fish? For a car ride through the countryside to listen to the birdies sing? Who knows, maybe even back to the White House? But only if they promise not to make him work so hard. As far as I am concerned, the Boss has already worked hard enough for his country. He has given it everything he has.

There is one thing I know for certain. When he does come, he will have a big biscuit. He will hold it up, and after I have done every trick in my bag—including saying *please* in my softest White House Voice—he will give me the biscuit. And it will be the tastiest biscuit any dog ever ate.

Until then, I will be patient, because I know that sooner or later, I will be back where I belong: five steps ahead of the Boss's wheelchair, leading the presidential parade as only a First Dog can do.

APPENDIX

A Man and His Scottie

In November 1940, at the time Fala went to live at the White House, Franklin Delano Roosevelt had just won a historic third term. Eight years earlier, when Roosevelt had first come to office, the country lay in shambles. The stock market had crashed, the banks had failed, millions were out of work, and people had lost faith in themselves and their government. Roosevelt took swift and decisive action to get the American people back on their feet. As he told them in his first inaugural speech, "The only thing we have to fear is fear itself."

Roosevelt was a man who knew a little something about overcoming fear.

He was the only child of Sara Delano and James Roosevelt, a man more than twice the age of his wife. For much of Franklin's youth, his father was unwell. He and his mother lived in the shadow of James's failing health. Perhaps this is when young Franklin learned to hide his feelings and to always appear upbeat. In boarding school at Groton, he was lonely and a little lost, spurned by the more popular boys. But he put a cheery face on things in his letters home. He studied hard and did his best even though he was neither a brilliant student nor an able athlete. He graduated and went on to attend Harvard University and Columbia Law School. On St. Patrick's Day 1905, he married a distant cousin, Eleanor, the favorite niece of President Teddy Roosevelt, who officiated at their wedding.

As politically ambitious as his cousin Teddy,

Franklin ran for and won a Democratic seat in the New York senate in 1910. Ten years later, he served under President Woodrow Wilson as assistant secretary of the navy. Then, in the summer of 1921, tragedy struck. He contracted poliomyelitis, a disease that paralyzed his legs. Many believed that his political career was over.

But Franklin was no quitter. He took up residence in Warm Springs, Georgia, which had a mineral spring that was said to have miraculous healing powers. While he never succeeded in regaining the use of his legs, he worked tirelessly, exercising to strengthen his arms and shoulders. He perfected a method of using his upper body to move his legs, encased in heavy steel. It looked like very painstaking walking, but Franklin jokingly called it "stumping."

When the 1924 Democratic National Convention rolled around, he was able to stump up to the podium to nominate the presidential candidate Al Smith as "the Happy Warrior." While the Happy Warrior failed to win office, Roosevelt was more successful four years later when he ran for governor of New York. It was a mere four years after this that he was elected president.

With the country in the depths of the Great Depression, it was a job few politicians wanted to touch, but Roosevelt couldn't wait to get to work. He moved swiftly "to wage war against the emergency" every bit as if "we were, in fact, invaded by a foreign foe." He passed laws to establish large public-works projects like dams, bridges, hospitals, and schools so that people would have jobs building them. He passed laws to protect farmers, to stabilize the economy, and to bring relief to the hungry and homeless. He gave workers more bargaining power and paid artists to make public sculptures, paint murals, and write plays. Over the next eight years, the laws, programs, and projects he put into effect were called the New Deal.

The New Deal was controversial. Some people thought it gave the federal government too much power. Other people felt that it wasn't working fast enough. It was the prospect of war in Europe and the looming Nazi threat that finally got America back on its feet. Now that there was a genuine outside foe to wage war against, Roosevelt was ready and raring to go.

Margaret "Daisy" Suckley worried about her beloved cousin Franklin. No other president in history except Washington and Lincoln had administered during such trying times. The way she saw it, Roosevelt was surrounded by enemies and critics, both abroad (Hitler, Mussolini, and Hirohito) and at home (his Republican rivals). What the president needed was a friend who would stand by his side and love him no matter what. She figured Big Boy fit the bill.

Big Boy was a third-generation American, having descended from Jamie, who was brought to America from Scotland by a wealthy banker. His mother was Keyfield Wendy. His sire was Peter the Reveller. The breeder, Mrs. August Kellogg of Westport, Connecticut, gave him as a gift to Daisy Suckley, understanding that, if the president approved, the dog would eventually go to live in the White House. After she had housebroken and trained him, Daisy took him for a trial meeting with the president at his home in Hyde Park, New York. The Scottie went on a picnic with the president and his staff, the secretary of agriculture, a U.S. senator, and assorted foreign visitors and dignitaries. Apparently, the little dog passed muster. Roosevelt renamed him Murray the Outlaw of Falahill, after a notorious Scottish ancestor. The dog quickly became known to one and all as Fala.

In November, following the election, Daisy brought Fala—by then eight months old—to the White House to live. From that day on, he seldom left the president's side. The Secret Service men liked to joke that an assassin trying to track down the president had only to look for the little black Scottie. Their nickname for Fala was the Informer.

FDR was the first truly public president. He held frequent press conferences at the White House. Over the radio, he kept the nation informed with regular Fireside Chats. When reporters met Fala and watched him do tricks for FDR, it was love at first sight. Fala began to show up in newspapers, newsreels, and political cartoons. Daisy wrote a children's book about him, in collaboration with Alice Dalgliesh, called *The True Story of Fala*. Based on the book, MGM made a short film, directed by Gunther von Fritsch, called *Fala: The President's Dog*. Both the book and the short were hits. At a time when war weighed heavily on all Americans, Fala and his frisky hijinks offered comic relief.

Fala was in the news almost as much as the president, hobnobbing with politicians and royalty and heads of state. He was seen accompanying FDR on his travels to international conferences in Canada and Mexico, to munitions plants and army bases, on fishing trips, and on jaunts around Hyde Park in FDR's sporty blue Ford. In addition to being president of Barkers for Britain, he was made an honorary private in the United States Army. American soldiers even used Fala's name as a secret password during the Battle of the Bulge as a way of separating friend from foe. Fala toys, cups, plates, and figurines were all the rage and today are collector's items.

FDR knew that appearances were important. Could the American people place their confidence in a crippled man to lead them out of Depression and into war? Roosevelt did not want to take any chances. He knew how important it was for him to appear not only cheerful and optimistic, but physically strong and able to stand on his own two feet. Considering how public this presidency was, it was nothing short of miraculous that the American people almost never saw the man sitting in a wheelchair, wearing his leg braces, or in any situation in which he appeared to be handicapped. An intimate family picnic in Hyde Park was one thing. At more public events, especially those covered by the media, he always appeared either standing or sitting in a chair, *but never in a wheelchair.* There was a conspiracy of silence with which the press cooperated. (And if they didn't, there was always a Secret Service man on hand to destroy the film.) It is possible that the joyful antics of Fala kept people's attention off the president and the often complex logistics of getting him from one place to another. The little Scottie dog might have served not only as a dear companion, but also as a strategic distraction.

There are very few pictures that show FDR in a wheelchair or wearing his braces. The Roosevelt monument, unveiled in Washington, D.C., in 1997, shows him wearing his signature wool navy cape, which concealed the wheelchair. The cape functions in the statue much as it did in life. In a way, the monument perpetuates the conspiracy of silence hiding the fact that the president who led the nation triumphantly through twelve of its most trying years was wheelchair-bound. It is also the only presidential monument that includes a dog.

Fala was with FDR on April 12, 1945, when he collapsed and died of a cerebral hemorrhage. He never lived to see the peace he had sought so steadfastly. He died a month before the Germans surrendered, ending the war in Europe, and four months before his successor, Harry Truman, ordered atomic bombs dropped on Hiroshima and Nagasaki, ending the war in the Pacific. People who were at the Little White House that day in April said that at the moment of FDR's passing, Fala started barking eerily and staring fixedly at something floating in midair. He moped for days afterward.

Roosevelt had told Daisy that he wanted her to

take care of Fala if anything ever happened to him. But Eleanor sent her son James to ask Daisy to let Fala remain at Hyde Park. She was quite fond of Fala. As much as Daisy loved Fala, she consented. After all, Fala had been the most popular First Dog of all time, and his place was with the First Lady. As a consolation, Daisy got her own Scottie, Button, with whom Fala later sired two pups.

Even though Fala was retired from public life, the public had not tired of Fala. Eleanor kept Americans abreast of his activities in her popular weekly newspaper column, "My Day." A second short film, *Fala at Hyde Park,* came out in 1945.

In spite of the ongoing attention given to Fala, Eleanor believed he never fully rebounded from the shock of losing his master. The happy-go-lucky Scottie seemed lost without FDR. In the end, Fala was reunited with his beloved Boss. When he died at the age of twelve, he was buried in the rose garden at Hyde Park, not far from his master's grave. He is the only dog ever to share a presidential burial site.

The Franklin D. Roosevelt Presidential Library and Museum website has extensive photographs, documents, and fun facts about the president, Fala, and Mrs. Roosevelt. It also has information about the Depression and the Second World War. The library and museum have a separate site for teachers that is rich in resources, with curriculum guides for students in third through twelfth grades. Go to:

- fdrlibrary.marist.edu/education

To find out more about Franklin Delano Roosevelt, go to:

- whitehouse.gov/about/presidents/franklind roosevelt

More About the Scottish Terrier

The Scottish terrier, or Scottie, was originally a working dog, bred by farmers in Scotland to hunt and kill rats, mice, and squirrels. It was the favorite breed of King James VI of Scotland, who promoted its popularity during the 1500s and 1600s. He sent six dogs overseas as a gift to the royal family of France. In 1680, the first Earl of Dumbarton nicknamed the breed the diehard, owing to its rugged looks and brave spirit.

Over the years, controversy raged between the English and the Scots as to the true nature of a Scottish terrier. The English owned and entered into competition what they claimed were Scottish terriers, but irate Scots insisted they were nothing of the kind. Och! They were said to be English terriers or Airedales or Dandie Dinmonts. Captain Gordon Murray, writing under the pen name of

Strathbogie in 1879, settled the squabble by laying out the exact standards, or traits, later used by the Scottish Terrier Club, founded in 1882.

John Naylor brought the Scottish terrier to America in 1883. The first one registered in this country was Dake, sired by one of Naylor's dogs. Scotties went on to become a popular breed, winning more Best in Show titles in the American Kennel Club Show than any other breed except the wirehaired terrier. Apart from Fala, there have been three other Scotties in the White House: Dwight D. Eisenhower's Skunky and George W. Bush's Barney and Miss Beazley.

The Scottie is a short-legged, big-headed little dog, standing ten inches tall at the shoulder and weighing between eighteen and twenty-two pounds. Roosevelt liked his Fala shaggy, and that's the way most Scottie owners prefer their dogs, with the fur on their beards, eyebrows, and legs allowed to grow long. Scotties come in black, brown, brindle (black and brown), white, and wheaten (tan).

Owning a Scottish Terrier

The Scottie is quick, alert, smart, and territorial. For a small dog, it has a loud bark, so it makes a great watchdog. With training, the Scottie is a good and loyal pet, but be aware that it has a mind of its own. And, as Fala did, it has personality to spare. If you make fun of it, it might get huffy and indignant. When you feel sad, it will do tricks to cheer you up. Yell at it, and it's liable to cover its head with shame. And if it finds a way to make you laugh, chances are it'll go for the laugh again and again. With those stubby legs, it's no distance runner, but it is a wonderful walking companion.

By nature it is a digger, so it will keep the garden free of squirrels and voles—and full of holes if you don't watch out. Since chasing after badgers and foxes is in its blood, caution should be taken when introducing it to cats. This shaggy creature requires regular grooming, but the good news is that it sheds very little.

If a Scottie is the right dog for you, make sure you go to a reputable breeder. Like many purebred dogs, the Scottie has its share of health issues. Scotties suffer from a high rate of bladder cancer and also can carry the gene for Von Willebrand's disease, a bleeding disorder. But a well-bred Scottie can bring you great joy and many years of happy companionship.

For more information, go to:

- akc.org/breeds/scottish_terrier/index.cfm
- stca.biz

A Word About Dogs and Car Safety

One of the more memorable photographs of Fala shows him with his head sticking out of a passenger-side window of FDR's sporty blue Ford. And this was, in fact, Fala's preferred way to travel. But these days we know a lot more about automobile safety than we did in the 1940s.

Today, seat belts are a mandatory feature of all cars, whereas they were almost unheard of in the 1940s. We also know now that it is dangerous to let our canine companions ride with their heads sticking out of open car windows. No matter how much they might enjoy themselves, it is not advisable to indulge them, for a number of very good reasons. They can get dust or dirt or pebbles in their eyes. The constantly blowing wind can cause irritation and even inflammation of their tender earflaps. There is even the very real possibility that, with a sharp turn or sudden stop, they might fall out of the window or break their neck on the window glass. And at the sight of a squirrel or cat or other dog, some dogs have been known to leap from moving cars.

So play it safe and don't let your dogs ride with their heads hanging out of open windows. Put them in a pet seat belt, behind a wire or mesh barrier, or in a travel crate. Crack a window and give dogs a wee taste of the breeze while keeping them safe and sound inside the car, because an important part of loving animals is protecting them from harm.

For more on pet auto safety, check out:

- aspca.org/pet-care/car-travel-tips
- humanesociety.org/animals/resources/tips
  /traveling_tips_pets_ships_planes_trains.html